E
MIL

Miller, Edna   81-87

Mousekin takes a
trip

DATE			
	5		
N-7	1		
	RA	2 - 2006	
R-2		NOV 2 - 2006	
12	FEB 0 5 2008		
6			
N-1			
4			
3			

© THE BAKER & TAYLOR CO.

Mousekin Takes A Trip

Mousekin Takes A Trip

81- 87

by Edna Miller

Prentice-Hall, Inc., Englewood Cliffs, N.J.

10   9   8   7   6   5   4   3

Printed in the United States of America •J

Prentice-Hall International, Inc., London
Prentice-Hall of Australia, Pty. Ltd., North Sydne
Prentice-Hall of Canada, Ltd., Toronto
Prentice-Hall of India Private Ltd., New Delhi
Prentice-Hall of Japan, Inc., Tokyo

Library of Congress Cataloging in Publication Data

Miller, Edna.
    Mousekin takes a trip.

    SUMMARY: While searching for food in a house o
wheels, a white-footed mouse takes an unexpected trip
to the desert and sees some unusual sights.
    1. Mouse—Legends and stories.   [1. Mice—Fictio
2. Deserts—Fiction]   I. Title.
PZ10.3.M5817Mk   [E]   75-35922
    ISBN 0–13–604363–1
    ISBN 0–13–604348–8 (pbk.)

To Lorraine and Ted

In early spring,
when rain-filled seeds begin to grow
and winter's store of food is gone,
a white-footed mouse is hungry.

Mousekin was hungry when he found the house
that stood near the woods in the clearing.
He didn't know, when he hopped inside
to search for a crumb or two,
that the door of the little house
would CLOSE
and carry him far away.

As Mousekin nibbled the food he found,
the room began to sway.
He hopped upon a window ledge
and blinked his eyes to see
trees and woodland creatures
disappear from view.

When the house rolled to the open road,
he saw strange things chase near.
Mousekin didn't wait to see them
pass and speed away.
He raced to a corner of the room
and made a hasty nest
of bits of paper, fluff and string
all pulled above his head.

Mousekin couldn't count the miles

nor all the days that passed.

He only knew he'd never been
so far from home before.

One night the door stood open
as he searched the room for food.
With a squeak,
he jumped to the ground below
and raced away to freedom.

The slipping sands of the desert floor
soon tired the little mouse.
There were no paths to follow;
no underbrush in which to hide.
Above him was the open sky;
no leafy branches hid the stars.
Strange figures loomed in darkness.
There were no forest smells.

When Mousekin could run no longer
he stopped and looked about.
Was that a beaded dragon?
A long-eared cat
with rings around its tail?

When something furry brushed beside him,
Mousekin dove for cover.
Beneath a sandy blanket,
and safely out of sight,
Mousekin closed his eyes and slept.

When morning came and Mousekin
woke, he saw the strangest land.
A huge round sun rose bright and
red straight from the desert floor.
Giant plants with outstretched
arms stood rooted to the ground.
There were clusters of waxy beaver
tails with thorns on every side.

Mousekin drummed his tiny paw
upon the desert sand.
(White-footed mice will drum their paw
when frightened or excited.)
Something near him in the sand
awakened with the sound.....

A horned toad lizard
appeared before him,
flicking the sand
from his scaly back.

Mousekin leaped into the air—
away from the awful creature.
The lizard didn't follow.
He breakfasted on ants.

Mousekin dove between some rocks.
round and weather-worn.
As he tried to squirm beneath one,
it stretched and walked away.
The armadillo wouldn't harm a mouse.
It hunted insects too.

The blazing sun had risen high.
It scorched the ground below.
Mousekin was hot and thirsty
when he spied a pool of water
shimmering on the sand.

The faster Mousekin ran toward it,
the farther the pool appeared to be.
He had never seen a mirage before
and didn't know the sun played tricks
on sparkling desert sands.

As he rested for a moment,
near a thorny pad,
Mousekin heard a munching sound.
He had heard that sound in the forest
and peeked out unafraid.

A desert tortoise snapped large chunks
of juicy prickly pear.
The tortoise was much larger
than turtles he had known.
The tortoise stopped his munching
just long enough to say,
"All desert plants have water stored
inside their waxy stems."
Mousekin tasted the juicy plant,
then nibbled hungrily.
With green plants holding wells of water
and food enough to eat
Mousekin knew he could survive
if he could find a shelter.

Halfway up a small saguaro,
Mousekin spied a hole;
the very same size a woodpecker makes
in the trunk of an old cherry tree.
He scampered up the fluted stem
'til he came to the opening
and hopped inside to rest.

From his room in the saguaro,
Mousekin watched the scene below.
There would be no need to venture far
with food outside his door.

He watched a desert mother feed her young
and a side-winder leave its pattern in the sand
'til a flash of lightning
and a clap of thunder
sent them racing for some cover.

The wind blew hard.
It blew dry grasses from afar.
It sent swirls of sand high into the air.
It sent an elf owl home.

Mousekin jumped and landed lightly
in a passing tumbleweed.
It bounced and rolled across the ground.

Mousekin rolled over and over,
looping and spinning about.
There was nothing to stop its onward rush,
pushed from behind by the wind.

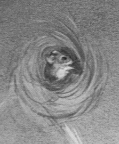

Until, in a sudden gust, it came to rest
against the house on wheels.
Its door, for a moment, opened
and Mousekin slipped inside.
In a corner he curled up in a furry ball.
He didn't hear the rain beat down.
He slept a long, long time.

When the room swayed, gently, once again,
Mousekin jumped to the sill.
The desert was changed as if by magic.
There was color everywhere!

Mousekin brushed the sand from his coat
as the little house rolled along.
When the sun went down in the western sky
he knew he was going home.

Home to a damp and shady nook
beside a stream in the forest;
where leafy branches shield the sky
and sunlight filters down
on fern and moss and a white-footed mouse
who had traveled so far away.